For Debbie,
with love from the legendary scooter man

First U.S. edition 2008

Library of Congress Cataloging-in-Publication Data is available.

Library of Congress Catalog Card Number 2006051857

ISBN 978-0-7636-3463-6

2 4 6 8 10 9 7 5 3 1

Printed in China

This book was typeset in Cochin.
The illustrations were done in watercolor and ink.

Candlewick Press
2067 Massachusetts Avenue
Cambridge, Massachusetts 02140

visit us at www.candlewick.com

Baby
Brains
and
ROBOMOM

Simon James

CANDLEWICK PRESS
CAMBRIDGE, MASSACHUSETTS

Before Baby Brains was born, Mrs. Brains ate lots of fish and nuts, which are good foods for brains.

She also played foreign languages on headphones and read out loud to the baby inside her tummy. Mr. and Mrs. Brains were hoping for a clever baby.

But when Baby Brains
was born, they were
amazed to see just how
clever he turned out to be.

When the hospital
scanned Baby
Brains's head,
they compared his
brain with a normal
baby's, and . . .

Memory bank

Personality

Language center

Math

Spare room

The senses

idea spot

Music area

more spare room

they were amazed
at the difference!

At home, Baby Brains
had no time for toys.
He preferred working
on the computer . . .

and doing experiments with his chemistry set.

But most of all, he loved designing new inventions.

Baby Brains invented
the first remote-controlled
self-rocking cradle.

He also invented the first
fully motorized stroller.

But despite his brilliant labor-saving inventions,
Baby Brains could see how tired his parents were
at the end of each day.

Once, his mom even fell asleep
during his bedtime story.

One night, Baby Brains stayed up inventing something
special to help Mr. and Mrs. Brains.

He was sure science and technology would have the answer.
It took him all night and well into the next morning.

Finally, at lunchtime, he was able to present Mrs. Brains with his most ambitious invention to date.

"It's RoboMom,"
 said Baby Brains.
"Gosh!" said Mrs. Brains.
"What does she do?"

"The ironing, for starters," said Baby Brains.

"Fantastic!" said Mrs. Brains.

RoboMom soon took over all the household chores.
She cooked the evening meal and cleaned up afterward.

"Wonderful!" said
Mrs. Brains.

The following day, RoboMom washed the car.

"Terrific!" said Mr. Brains.

By the weekend,
RoboMom had
even taken over
looking after
the baby.

First she changed Baby Brains's diaper.
But Baby Brains preferred his mom to do that.

Later she gave
Baby Brains a bath.
But Baby Brains
preferred his dad
to do that.

The worst was to come when RoboMom insisted on putting Baby Brains to bed. "Don't let the RoboBugs bite," said RoboMom.

"She's doing too much," said Mrs. Brains. "And what's all that smoke coming out of her head?" said Mr. Brains.

The next morning, instead of cereal, RoboMom served
nuts and bolts in engine oil for breakfast.
"Something is wrong," said Mr. Brains.
"I think I'll have a yogurt," said Mrs. Brains.

Later, RoboMom washed Baby Brains in the kitchen sink with all the dishes!

Then she hung him out to dry on the line.

Baby Brains tried
to wriggle free,
but the clothespins
held him in place.

He started to
sway in the breeze
along with the
laundry.

Baby Brains
began to cry.
"I want my mommy!"
he called.

Mrs. Brains was upstairs when she heard her baby calling.
She looked out of the window and could hardly believe her eyes.

She raced
down the stairs,
through the kitchen,

and into the yard.
She grabbed hold of her baby.

"Quick, Mom!"
said Baby Brains.
"I think
RoboMom is
about to . . .

EXPLODE!"

As the smoke cleared, Mrs. Brains held her baby tight.

"Thanks, Mom," said Baby Brains.

That night, everyone helped cook dinner
and clean up afterward.

Later, Mr. and Mrs. Brains put Baby Brains to bed.
It was nice to do things together again.

Of course,

Baby Brains didn't stop inventing.

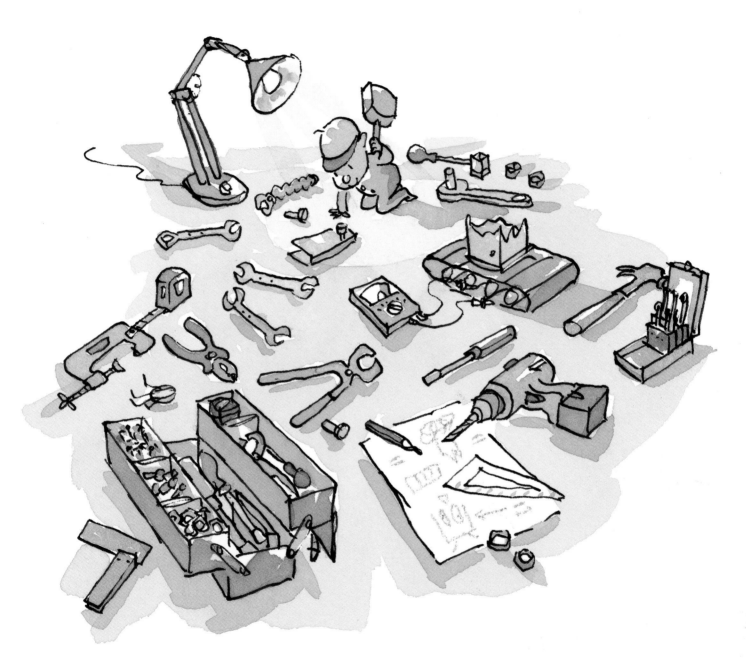

Soon he came up with something he was sure

his mom and dad would enjoy.

It was the new, improved . . .

RoboMom 2!

The End